THINGS YOU SHOULD KNOW ABOUT

BABY ANIMALS

By Steve Parker
Illustrated by Ian Jackson

Miles Kelly
PUBLISHING

First published in 2004 by
Miles Kelly Publishing Ltd
Bardfield Centre
Great Bardfield
Essex, CM7 4SL

Copyright © Miles Kelly Publishing Ltd 2004

10 9 8 7 6 5 4 3 2 1

Editorial Director: Anne Marshall
Project Editor: Belinda Gallagher
Editorial Assistant: Lisa Clayden
Designer: Herring Bone Design
Artwork Commissioning: Bethany Walker
Production: Estela Godoy
Indexer: Jane Parker

ISBN 1-84236-195-3

Printed in China

www.mileskelly.net
info@mileskelly.net

British Library Cataloguing-in-Publication Data
A catalogue record for this book is available
from the British Library

Contents

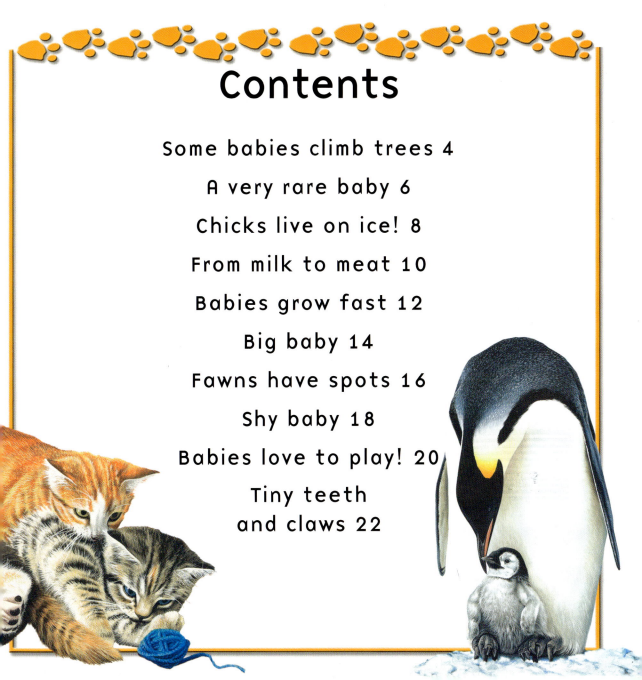

1 Some babies climb tree

Orang facts
• There are two kinds of orangs found in Borneo and Sumatra, Southeast Asia.
• They are very rare, and are protected by law.
• 'Orang-utan' means 'mystery man of the woods'.

A baby **ORANG-UTAN** is like a baby human, except hairier! It sleeps a lot, cries when hungry or frightened, and goes to the toilet where it wants. But the mother orang is very caring and protects her baby from enemies — including huge eagles!

As the young orang grows, it begins to try different foods. It will eat mainly fruits, also flowers and buds, with the odd snack of a juicy lizard or bird's egg.

Orangs usually live alone, except for a mother and baby. They may stay together for as long as eight years.

Orang-utans live in trees all their lives. They are expert climbers because they have four 'hands' – their feet and toes grasp almost as well as their hands and fingers.

Like all baby mammals, the young orang feeds on its mother's milk. But, compared to other mammals, it does this for a very long time – three years or more!

Bend a branch!

The male orang is twice as big as the female. At 80 kilograms, he is the world's heaviest tree-living creature.

2 A very rare baby

Panda facts
- Pandas live only in south and west China.
- There are less than 1000 left in the wild.

A newborn **GIANT PANDA** cub is not a giant. It is smaller than your hand, white all over, has almost no fur, and its eyes are tightly closed! But the cub grows quickly. By six weeks old it can leave its den and follow its mother. By six months old it is eating its life-long favourite food, bamboo.

The baby panda is born in a den, in a cave or hollow tree. The mother leaves it twice daily, for an hour or two, for food and water.

The panda appears to have a sixth finger. But this is really a long, bendy part of its wrist. It is used to hold bamboo stems and leaves.

Panda meals are very boring – bamboo, bamboo and more bamboo. But sometimes they eat fruits, eggs, insects and even the meat from a dead animal.

Hi, panda-face!

Make this famous animal face from white card, with four black circles. Can people guess what you are?

It is hard for young pandas to find somewhere to set up home. Their bamboo forests are being cut down to make way for farmland.

3 Chicks live on ice!

Penguin facts

- The 17 kinds of penguin all live in the far south, around Antarctica.
- Penguins are not hunted by polar bears because these live in the far north!

No baby grows up in a colder place than the **EMPEROR PENGUIN** chick. It is −50 degrees Celsius in icy Antarctica, colder than a food deep-freezer. Luckily the chick has its father to keep it warm.

Older chicks grow fluffy down feathers. They huddle together for extra warmth in the icy wind.

Father penguins shelter younger chicks in their belly feathers.

The penguin chick cheeps and pecks its parent's beak. This makes the parent bring up food from its stomach. The meal is smelly, half-rotted fish and lumps of slimy squid.

After two months at sea catching food such as shrimplike krill, the mother penguin returns to her baby. Now the father can go off to feed.

Who's taller?

The emperor penguin is the biggest penguin. It is 120 centimetres in height. How tall are you?

From milk to meat

Wolf facts

- Wolves live in almost all northern lands.
- A big wolf is 2 metres long, including its bushy tail, and weighs 60 kilograms.

For the first few weeks, baby **GREY WOLVES** stay inside. They are safe in their den, in a cave or burrow. Their mother feeds them on milk. Then they begin to leave the den and start to eat meat.

The mother wolf usually has three to five cubs. In rare cases she may have as many as ten!

The cubs nip, pounce, scramble and tumble. Their 'play' is practice for when they grow up to hunt prey.

Wolf cubs are brought their first meaty meals not only by their mother, but by their father too – and by other members of the pack.

Howlin' wolf

Wolves do not really howl at the Moon. They are telling other wolves: 'I'm here!'

5 Babies grow fast

Seal facts

- A newborn seal pup weighs 12 kilograms – four times more than a human baby!
- It grows faster than almost any other animal, doubling its weight in five days!

The **HARP SEAL** pup lives in the cold, white wilderness of the Arctic. This baby is surrounded by snow, ice and freezing cold sea — as well as hungry predators such as polar bears and wolves. The pup lies perfectly still, hoping its thick, white fur will keep it warm and unnoticed.

The pup's fur is yellow at birth. It soon becomes a 'whitecoat' for a few weeks. Then it grows a new, darker fur coat.

If a pup cannot find its mother, it wails and cries like a human baby.

A harp seal pup is a baby for only two weeks. Then its mother stops feeding it on milk, plunges into the sea, and is gone. The pup must learn to swim, dive and catch fish – fast!

Harp seals eat mainly fish such as herring, cod and capelin. They might try a snack of squid.

Down and down

Harp seals can dive more than 300 metres and stay underwater for half an hour!

Big baby

Elephant facts

• The African elephant is the largest land animal, weighing up to 8 tonnes.

• A big elephant eats 300 kilograms of grass and other plants daily – which is the weight of five full-grown people!

An **ELEPHANT** baby has the world's biggest, strongest family for protection – not only its mother, but also older sisters, aunties, and even grandmother, who leads the whole herd!

For the first year or two, the calf hardly strays more than a metre or two from its mother's legs.

The mother constantly touches her baby with her trunk. If she is busy feeding, an older sister or aunt 'babysits' and keeps the calf out of danger.

The baby feeds on its mother's milk for up to four years.

Cool, mum!

When a baby elephant wants to rest, its mother stands so that her shadow keeps the baby shaded and cool.

A young male elephant leaves the main herd at about 10 to 12 years of age. He teams up with other young males to form a smaller herd.

7 Fawns have spots

Deer facts
• The biggest deer mother, the moose, has the heaviest fawn. It weighs 15 kilograms.
• Only one type of female deer has antlers – the caribou or reindeer.

As the midsummer sun shines through leaves and twigs, it forms light spots on the woodland floor – just like the spots on a fawn's coat. The **FAWN** lies still and silent under a bush. Its mother is nearby, feeding and watching. She comes to her fawn for a few minutes, two or three times each day.

The doe (mother deer) visits her baby briefly, to feed it on her milk. Then she goes back to the main group, or herd.

The fawn's coat is dappled, with white spots on brown fur. It blends in with patches of sunlight on the ground, so the fawn is very difficult to see.

Big-head!
A buck is a full-grown male deer. He grows huge antlers each summer. They fall off in late winter.

The fawn has huge ears, big eyes and a keen nose to detect danger. If an enemy comes too near, the fawn jumps up and bounds away through the trees.

This fawn is a fallow deer. Female fallow deer do not have antlers. Males begin to grow them at about two years old.

The fawn stays hidden for a few weeks, visited by its mother. Then it joins the herd and begins to eat leaves.

17

8 Shy baby

Kangaroo facts

• When a joey is born, it is one of the tiniest mammal babies.

A baby kangaroo is called a **JOEY**. For the first six months its feet never touch the ground! It lives in its mother's pocket-shaped pouch and feeds on her milk. Gradually, the joey grows strong enough to leave the pouch and explore. But if danger appears, it soon hops back in again.

• At birth, it is smaller than your little finger, with no fur, and closed eyes.

A young joey is very shy. It rushes back to the pouch every minute! Soon it becomes bolder and stays out of the pouch longer.

Kangaroos live in very dry places in Australia, eating grass and leaves. They can go for days without water.

The older joey still pops its head into its mother's pouch to feed on her milk, until it is almost a year old.

The mother kangaroo has to clean her pouch often, using her hand claws, teeth and tongue. She throws out bits of dirt and fur that her joey leaves behind – and its droppings too!

Hop-hop-hop

Can you hop like a kangaroo? Keep your feet together, knees bent, and hands held up like paws.

When the joey is eight months old it leaves the pouch – and never comes back. But it still stays near its mother.

9 Babies love to play!

Otter facts

• Most animals have babies in spring or summer, but mother otters can give birth at any time of the year.

• The kits cannot open their eyes until they are four weeks old.

Many youngsters like to play – especially **OTTER** babies! They roll, tumble and jump in the riverbank mud. Sometimes they have pretend fights. But this 'play' is practice for when the otter babies, called kits, have to hunt their own food.

The kits stay in their burrow, called a holt, for more than two months. Their mother feeds them on her milk. When they are three months old, she leads them out to the riverbank, where they play and learn to swim.

By the time the kits are four months old they can catch their own small prey, such as fish, baby frogs and waterbird chicks.

Young otters are also called cubs or pups.

Lazy daysy

After a big meal, the otter spends a day or two lazing on a bare patch of ground, called its 'couch' or 'sofa'.

Kitten facts

• All kittens have grey-blue eyes. These change to the adult colour at 12 weeks.

• A kitten has two sets of teeth. The first set grow by eight weeks, the second after 12 weeks.

A mother cat is very busy. She has to feed her **KITTENS** on her milk, keep them warm, lick them clean every day, let them clamber all over her and stop them wandering into danger. She may have ten or more babies to care for!

Like a human baby, a kitten learns to crawl first. By about four weeks old it can walk. A week later it is running and jumping, but it may still fall over!

A kitten's eyes are closed for the first week of life. They are fully open by about three weeks.

A kitten feeds on its mother's milk for about eight weeks. It begins to eat other foods at three weeks.

The kittens sniff and rub their mother often. They can recognize each other by smell, even in total darkness.

Kittens should stay with their mother until they are eight weeks old.

Popular pets

Some years ago, dogs were the most popular pets. Now cats have taken over. How many pet cats do you know?

Index

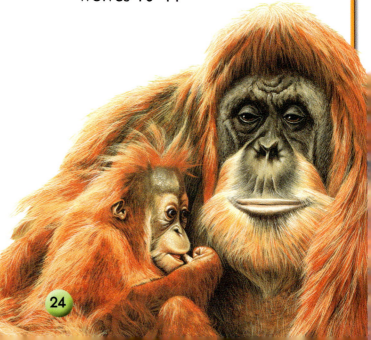